# Gary Grasshopper
# Helps Harry Hear

Written by Connie Amarel
Illustrated by Swapan Debnath

**ISBN 978-1-61225-288-9**

Published by Mirror Publishing
Milwaukee, WI 53214


Printed in the USA.

This book is dedicated to the hearing impaired with hope that they will seek out and find a wonderful audiologist/hearing doctor who can improve their hearing immensely. It is also dedicated to Dr. Jeffrey Danhauer, Audiologist extraordinaire, for suggesting this book and providing invaluable input, and to his granddaughters Lane and Reese. It is dedicated to Nicholas and Kai, two of the brightest and sweetest boys I've ever met. Many thanks to my dear friend Alan for his excellent suggestions, to my wonderful publisher Neal and amazingly talented illustrator Swapan. Much love and appreciation to my mother June Palette Rausch for inspiring me with the stories she told my sister and me when we were young and to my family for their endless love and support.

Gary Grasshopper grinned from ear to ear. The first day of school had finally arrived. He was excited to see the other students and his teacher.

Gary had enjoyed summer vacation and especially having his best friend, Freddie Firefly, come to visit him for two weeks. He had such a great time with Freddie. Gary missed him so much after he went home. He knew Freddie would be excited about school too. Gary quickly ate breakfast and then packed his lunch and put it in his new backpack.

He hopped out the door and down the sidewalk. He was meeting Buster, Inchy and Tommy at the park. They laughed and talked all the way to school. At school they saw the other students. They waved at some, hugged others and then headed to the classroom.

Their teacher, Mr. Nicholas Nightcrawler, greeted each of them at the door with a smile. When Gary hopped by, Mr. Nightcrawler asked if he could speak with Gary before class started. He had a favor to ask him. Mr. Nightcrawler knew that Gary was one of the kindest and smartest students at the school.

He told Gary that there was a new student named Harry Horsefly that had moved from a school in another town. Mr. Nightcrawler said that Harry was very shy and he hardly ever talked. He asked Gary if he would show Harry around the school and introduce him to the other students. Gary said he would be happy to.

Gary went over to Harry and introduced himself. He told Harry that at recess he could show him around the school. Gary asked Harry if he would like to sit with him and his friends at lunchtime. Harry didn't answer Gary, so Gary asked him again speaking much louder. This time Harry heard Gary and said he would like to join him and his friends at lunchtime.

Gary liked Harry a lot and thought he was really nice. Buster, Inchy and Tommy liked Harry a lot too.

They noticed that when they asked Harry a question, most of the time he would shrug his shoulders but he didn't answer.

When they talked to Harry they would have to repeat what they said, sometimes two or three times, talking louder each time.

Harry told them his ears were plugged and that was why he couldn't hear them.

In class when Mr. Nightcrawler asked Harry a question, Harry would shrug his shoulders because he couldn't hear what his teacher was asking him. Some of the other students wouldn't talk to Harry because he couldn't hear. They didn't ask him to play games with them either. This made Harry very sad.

Gary suddenly realized that the reason Harry was so shy was because he couldn't hear. If he couldn't hear, that would explain why he couldn't answer questions and why everything that was said to him had to be repeated loudly. Gary told Harry that he thought he should make an appointment to have his ears checked.

He said there was a wonderful ear doctor in town named Dr. Sky Squirrel. Gary was sure Dr. Squirrel would be able to help Harry. Harry said he was afraid to see Dr. Squirrel. He didn't know what Dr. Squirrel would do to him. Gary told Harry that he would go to the appointment with him and stay while he had his exam.

They went to the appointment on Saturday morning. The receptionist, Lane Ladybug, Lisa Ladybug's cousin, greeted them with a warm smile and asked them to fill out an information sheet. She told them to sit in the Waiting Room until the medical assistant, Reese Raccoon, came to take them to an Exam Room where they would meet Dr. Squirrel.

In a few minutes Reese Raccoon entered the Waiting Room and asked Harry and Gary to follow her to the Exam Room. In the Exam Room she asked Harry a few questions. She had to repeat the questions loudly so Harry could hear what she was saying. She wrote some notes in a chart. She told them that Dr. Squirrel would be in soon and left the Exam Room.

Dr. Squirrel came into the Exam Room and said a cheery hello. He introduced himself to Harry and thanked Gary for bringing Harry to his office. Dr. Squirrel told Harry he would like to do some tests on his ears. He described the tests and how they would be done. He explained how these tests were an important way to check for hearing loss.

Harry thought the tests were really fun and almost seemed like playing a video game. Dr. Squirrel did several tests and then told Harry the results. The tests showed that his hearing levels in both ears were very low. Dr. Squirrel told Harry that he would need hearing aids.

He explained that with the hearing aids Harry would be able to hear much better. Dr. Squirrel fit both ears with new hearing aids. After he had gently placed the hearing aids in each ear, he asked Harry how he liked his new school.

Harry quickly answered that he liked his new school and especially his new friend Gary Grasshopper. He told Dr. Squirrel about some of the students not wanting to play with him because he couldn't hear. Harry then asked Dr. Squirrel why he was talking so loudly. That made Dr. Squirrel happy because he knew the hearing aids were helping Harry hear.

Dr. Squirrel dropped his pen on the floor and the sound made Harry jump. They all laughed with joy because Harry could hear so well. Harry couldn't believe all the new sounds he was hearing. He could even hear Reese Raccoon walking down the hallway. Dr. Squirrel showed Harry how to take care of his hearing aids. He also showed him how to put them in his ears properly.

Harry put them in and took them out several times. It was very easy for him to do this. The hearing aids fit so well that you couldn't even see them. Dr. Squirrel gave Harry a case to put them in before he went to bed and also showed him the proper way to clean them.

When the appointment was over Harry hugged Dr. Squirrel and thanked him for helping him hear and then hugged Gary. After they left the office, Gary and Harry talked all the way home. Gary never had to repeat even one word. Harry was so excited about all the new sounds he could hear. He could hear birds chirping and leaves rustling on the trees.

When Harry went to school on Monday he could hear everything that Mr. Nightcrawler was saying. Buster, Inchy and Tommy were so happy for Harry and so thankful that Gary took him to see Dr. Squirrel. Mr. Nightcrawler was happy too and thanked Gary.

At lunchtime they all sat together at a big table. Gary smiled proudly as he watched Harry talking with the other students and answering their questions. Harry wasn't shy anymore because he could hear everything that was being said to him.

The other students liked talking with Harry now. They even asked him to join them when they played games. Harry was so happy to be able to hear them.

Harry loved going to school now that he was able to hear. He loved raising his hand to answer when Mr. Nightcrawler asked a question.

Most of all Harry loved his new friend Gary Grasshopper.
It was because of Gary's help that he could hear. He knew
they would be friends forever.

CPSIA information can be obtained at www.ICGtesting.com
Printed in the USA
LVIW01n0702110216
474625LV00003B/7